Little, Brown and Company

Hachette Book Group
237 Park Avenue, New York, NY 10017
Visit our website at lb-kids.com

Little, Brown and Company is a division of Hachette Book Group, Inc.
The Little, Brown name and logo are trademarks of
Hachette Book Group, Inc.

The publisher is not responsible for websites (or their content)
that are not owned by the publisher.

First Edition: March 2014

Library of Congress Control Number: 2013956687

ISBN 978-0-316-28333-5

10 9 8 7 6 5 4 3 2 1

RRD-C

Printed in the United States of America

The Chapter Book

Adapted by Stacia Deutsch

LITTLE, BROWN AND COMPANY
New York   Boston

Chapter One

Beyond London, past the second star to the right and straight on 'til morning, lay the glistening hills of Never Land. Above the meadows of Pixie Hollow, graceful fairies flitted across the blue sky.

But not Zarina.

She walked into Sunflower Meadow, where Rosetta, Silvermist, and Iridessa were working together to grow a lush field of flowers. Each fairy has their own special talent, which tells what their tasks are.

"There we go," Rosetta said as she planted seeds. Silvermist watered the soil.

"Little bit of sun." Iridessa added her touch,

then, noticing her friend Zarina, she said, "Oh, look!"

Rosetta gazed up and, seeing that Zarina was traveling on foot instead of flying, remarked, "Hey, Zarina. Out of pixie dust again, sugar?"

Zarina shrugged. Her red hair glistened in the sunlight. "You know me, Rosetta."

"I could give you some tips on conserving your supply," Iridessa suggested.

"I may just take you up on that, Dessa," Zarina said as she hurried out of the garden.

Silvermist shook her head. "A dust-keeper fairy who's always out of pixie dust."

"Ironic, isn't it?" Rosetta replied.

Zarina walked quickly through animal-fairy headquarters, where Fawn was busy bathing a couple of baby birds.

"Lift that wing! Right there—nice!" Fawn said to the birds. "Okay. Rinse time. Time to dry." The birds moved past Fawn's cleaning station to where Vidia was drying them with a soft gust of wind.

Zarina scurried by.

"Hey, Z! Wings okay?" Fawn called out.

"Just enjoying a stroll, but thanks, Fawn! Nice wind, Vidia!" She hurried away.

"Thanks." Vidia looked up from the birdbath. Then she asked Fawn, "What's a *stroll*?"

Zarina could see the Pixie Dust Tree in the distance.

"Oh no!" At the sound of a whistle signaling the start of her shift at the Pixie Dust Depot, she picked up her pace and jogged the rest of the way.

After stamping her fairy card, Zarina entered the pixie dust distribution area and slid down a rope to the assembly line area. Her work smock had a large *Z* in the center of it. She slipped it on, blew the hair out of her eyes, and took her place in the distribution line without a moment to spare.

Terence the sparrow man—what male fairies are called—blew his kazoo, marking the start of the workday. The assembly line began to roll. Pixie dust swirled around a central vat, funneled down into barrels, and then dropped gently onto leaves, where the measuring dust-keepers made sure there was just the right amount.

Zarina's station came next. As each package went by, she leaned in and studied the contents before wrapping the leaves into neat dust-filled packages.

"Uh." The dust-keeper next to Zarina pointed at Zarina's bangs, which were now floating up thanks to the pixie dust she'd sprinkled on them.

Zarina considered her hair. "We put the dust in the bags, and the bags stay there, right? And yet, we sprinkle dust on top of something, and it floats." She put a pinch of dust on her ponytail. The hair rose up toward the sky.

Suddenly, everyone in the line paused, pixie dust packages in hand.

The dust-keeper said, "Well, that's just how pixie dust works."

While everyone else seemed to accept that answer, Zarina didn't. She asked, "Well, yes, I know, but *why* is the question...isn't it?"

No one answered.

"Know what I mean? Not even a little? Never once had the thought?" Zarina asked them.

The dust-keepers still stared at her blankly.

Fairy Gary, the head dust-keeper, entered the factory floor, along with his assistant, Terence.

"Good morning, dust-keepers!" Fairy Gary greeted everyone.

Zarina shook the pixie dust out of her hair and muttered, "Oh!"

"All right, let's see, on Blue Dust Duty today, we have..." Gary looked at Terence. "What were we on?"

Terence looked at his list. "Y."

"Ah yes, Yvette." Gary glanced around.

"Yvette's out for the day, Fairy Gary. Her dust-keeper elbow flared up again," a fairy reported.

"That's fantastic!" Zarina suddenly shouted, then softened. "I mean, poor, poor Yvette."

"Well, that brings us to—" Fairy Gary stared at the list.

Zarina pointed to the *Z* on her apron. "Z."

"Z," Fairy Gary echoed with a long sigh. "Zarina, you're up."

"Uh-oh," a dust-keeper muttered as Zarina left the assembly area with Fairy Gary.

Zarina followed Fairy Gary into the Blue Pixie Dust Vault.

"I mean, one day early. It's so exciting," Zarina said happily. She stopped talking as Gary opened a fancy chest with a secret combination lock.

"Six clicks to the right...." Zarina watched him carefully, reciting the code from memory.

"Yes," Gary said. "Thank you."

The lid slid open.

"Whoa," Zarina gasped.

Inside the chest was the super-rare, amazing, sparkling Blue Pixie Dust. Blue Dust strengthened the Pixie Dust Tree and helped the tree make enough golden pixie dust for all the fairies in Pixie Hollow.

With their daily ration of pixie dust, fairies could fly and make magic. Pixie dust was extremely important, and adding Blue Dust to the tree was a huge responsibility.

Zarina took the job seriously. She slowly collected blue flecks into a clear glass vial.

Fairy Gary watched her. "Careful now: After last time, I am sure I don't have to remind you just how potent and powerful this—"

"No touching. I promise," Zarina said.

"Attagirl. All right, then, exactly twenty-six specks," Gary reminded her.

"But why twenty-six?" Zarina asked.

Gary sighed. "And here we go...."

"Why not twenty-five? What would happen if we put in, say, twenty-seven?"

"Zarina, you're the most inquisitive fairy I've ever known." Gary changed his mind. "Correction: It's a tie. Let's just say you're the Tinker Bell of dust-keepers."

"Why do you say that like it's a bad thing?" Zarina asked.

"Because we don't work with twigs and acorn caps. We work with pixie dust. It's our lifeblood." He paused before reminding her, "There's no room for error."

Fairy Gary and Zarina entered the boughs of the Pixie Dust Tree. The tree glowed as it made golden pixie dust. Zarina could see that the usual trickle of pixie dust was slow and weak.

Zarina handed Fairy Gary the vial. Fairy Gary poured the dust into a beautiful wood-and-glass container, refilling the tree's well with the precious blue flakes.

"Blue Dust—one of nature's mightiest multipliers—takes the golden dust from a trickle to a roar...." Gary said.

Zarina stood behind Gary and watched as the Blue Dust dropped speck by speck into the golden dust. The stream of golden dust grew bigger and brighter than before, cascading in a waterfall down the side of the tree.

"No matter how many times I see it—just, wow!" Zarina said. She thought it was beautiful.

"Indeed," Gary agreed.

Zarina knew that Blue Pixie Dust was created when the light of the Blue Moon shone through a moonstone at exactly ninety degrees. That's why the Blue Dust was so rare and precious, but still, Zarina wondered about other possibilities.

She asked Gary, "But, if there's Blue Dust, why *can't* there be other colors?"

"Because there aren't," Gary answered.

"And maybe those other colors do other things. What if there was—I don't know— purple? What if there's pink?" Zarina asked.

Fairy Gary chuckled. "The day someone finds pink pixie dust is the day I trade in my kilt for trousers."

Zarina's eyes lit up. "Well, what if we don't find it? What if we *make* it?"

Fairy Gary looked at her in a serious way. "Listen carefully, Zarina: We do not tamper with pixie dust; it is far too powerful."

"But if we don't, we'll never fully understand what it's capable of," Zarina said.

"That is not our job. We're dust-keepers," Gary told her. "We nurture the dust, maintain it, measure it, package it, and distribute it. A beautiful tradition, day in, day out, passed from one generation to the next to the next to the next."

Fairy Gary continued, but Zarina wasn't listening. She'd taken off her bracelet and dipped it into the well of golden dust. She watched as it rose into the air, and then flicked it with her finger into the path of the Blue Pixie Dust.

The combination of Blue Dust and golden dust supercharged her bracelet! Like a torpedo, the bracelet shot up. It bounced around the tree, ping-ponging off the limbs of the tree until— WHACK—it hit Fairy Gary in the face.

"Oh no. Fairy Gary! Are you okay?" Zarina asked.

Gary grunted.

"Technically, I didn't touch it this time."
Zarina frowned.

Gary simply took her bracelet away. He
removed the empty Blue Dust vial from the tree
receptacle and held it toward Zarina.

"The cap." He said it, and Zarina put the
lid on the vial. Then Gary lectured her, "Let
me be absolutely clear, Zarina: Dust-keepers are
forbidden to tamper with pixie dust."

With that, he flew away, leaving Zarina alone
at the tree.

Chapter Two

Z arina felt sad as she walked home.

Inside her small house, a curtain divided the living room from her research laboratory. She pulled back the curtain and put her daily ration of pixie dust into a large container that was already three-quarters full of dust.

She hadn't been using her ration of dust to fly because each fleck was important to her science.

Inside her journal, Zarina had detailed dozens of experiments. She'd written the same thing every time: "NO RESULT"..."NO RESULT"... "NO RESULT."

Zarina dropped her head to the table in frustration. A single speck of Blue Pixie Dust fell out of her hair. She picked it up and stared at it. Suddenly, inspiration struck!

She opened her journal and read. "Hmmm, light talent: two parts sunflower seed, a dash of moonflower, golden dust…"

Using a magnifying glass and a small blade, she took a sliver off the Blue Dust flake and mixed it with the other ingredients, chopping, mixing, and heating until—the golden dust turned orange!

"It worked!" Zarina exclaimed.

She reached out with a bit of the new dust on her fingers. The moonlight came through the window, and strangely, the beam changed directions when it touched Zarina's hand. Startled, she quickly brushed off the dust. This time when she touched the moonbeam, her hand passed right through.

Zarina jumped up and ran all the way to Tink's house.

She pounded on the door.

Tink was covered in work grease from her latest project. "Oh, hey, Zarina! What brings you here?"

Zarina explained, "Tinker Bell, remember how you were the first one to use Lost Things and everyone thought you were kind of crazy?"

"I believe Fairy Mary called them 'junk,'" Tink admitted.

"Exactly, but now even she uses them, and tinkering's better than ever!"

"Well, that's nice of you to—" Tink said.

"And remember how you crossed the winter border when you knew it wasn't allowed, but you just had to anyway?" Zarina asked.

"I like to think it was more of a gray area," Tink said.

"Good. Now, keep that in mind." She grabbed Tink's hand and dragged her to her house.

Tink was shocked as she watched Zarina bend a

moonbeam. "You're bending light?! But you're not a light fairy; you're a dust-keeper!"

"Amazing, right?" Zarina grinned.

"But how?" Tink asked.

Zarina showed her the orange dust on her hands.

"Whoa. You found orange pixie dust?!" Tink asked.

"No, Tink. I *made* orange pixie dust."

"That's never been done before." Tink stared at Zarina in shock.

"I knew you'd understand." Zarina gathered her supplies. "Now I can finally figure out everything pixie dust is capable of."

As Zarina dashed around, Tink flipped through Zarina's lab book.

"What does Fairy Gary think about all this?" Tink asked. She was worried.

"Uh, he doesn't know," Zarina admitted.

"What?" Tinker Bell asked.

As Tink watched, Zarina grabbed trimmings of a purple feather and a measuring cup filled with pixie dust. She combined them in a pan.

"He doesn't really think we should tamper with pixie dust," Zarina said as she handed Tink a spoon. "Do you mind stirring?"

"Uh...okay..." Tink took the spoon.

"I guess he thinks it's just too powerful." Zarina shrugged.

Tinker Bell could not believe her ears. She stopped stirring and stared at Zarina.

"Oh, you can't stop." Zarina pointed at the pan. At her worktable, Zarina picked up the smallest sliver from the Blue Dust flake.

"Is that Blue Dust?" Tink couldn't believe her eyes. "You're doing this with Blue Dust?!"

"Yes," Zarina replied casually. "And it just takes the tiniest bit. Can you believe it?" She put on safety goggles and told Tink to back up.

She dropped in the sliver and then—POP! A mini explosion rattled Tink's pan.

Tinker Bell screamed.

Zarina leaned in to investigate, putting her finger in the mixture. Her hand was coated in purple dust. "Purple pixie dust!"

She wiggled her fingers. A giant gust of wind swirled around the room.

"Wind! Purple equals fast-flying talent!" Zarina was excited. Papers flew everywhere.

Tink ducked, but not before a flower hit her in the face.

Zarina took the flower. "Garden talent next!" She rushed to her journal to try to crack pink pixie dust.

"Zarina," Tink warned, "you think maybe you should slow down a little bit?"

Zarina put flower petals in a beaker filled with water. "Pink pixie dust for optimal plant growth. A ratio of five pieces of petal for every three drops of extract."

Tink looked in the pan. "Should it be bubbling like that?"

"Mmmm." Zarina considered it. She poured the pink mixture into a bowl of pixie dust and added two slivers of the Blue Dust flake.

"Two?" Tink questioned, alarmed.

"You're adding two?"

"Uh-huh," Zarina agreed.

The liquid boiled and popped violently until it exploded. Dust covered Zarina's face.

"Are you okay?" Tink asked.

Zarina rubbed the dust off. It was pink. "Tinker Fairy Gary some trousers, cuz I just made pink pixie dust!" She laughed.

Zarina grinned as she cradled the bowl of pink dust.

"This seems really dangerous," Tink said.

Ignoring the warning, Zarina grabbed a small plant. "Do you know what this means, Tink? I've finally found *my* Lost Things! Dust-keeping will change forever."

Tink frowned. "Zarina, I really think you should stop!"

"What?!" Zarina was stunned as she turned around to face her friend. As she rotated, she spilled the entire bowl of pink dust on a sapling.

The sapling began growing fast. Too fast. BOOM!

Its roots burst out of the pot. They spread across the house and cracked through the floor.

"Oh no...no, no, no!" Zarina shouted, seeing what she'd done.

Tink and Zarina ran as Zarina's entire house was lifted up, high into the air!

All through Pixie Hollow, homes were being picked up by wild vines.

At the Pixie Dust Depot, Terence and Fairy Gary tried to fight back the out-of-control plant.

"Oh no! Oh, good golly! No, no." Gary was no match for their strength. The roots pushed him back, breaking through and completely destroying the Dust Depot.

After crawling out from the rubble, Fairy Gary bent down and touched the ground. When he stood again, his finger was coated in pink pixie dust.

Zarina raced to the demolished Depot and looked at the devastation around her: vines, stems, and flowers had grown up and over everything.

A crowd gathered in town. Fairy Gary was there with the dust-keepers, Zarina's friends, and Queen Clarion.

"How did this happen?" the queen asked.

Zarina sighed sadly.

"Tink, are you okay?" Silvermist asked Tink.

"Yeah," Tink said, dusting off her dress.

"Who grew these?" Rosetta surveyed the plants.

But Gary knew the answer to that question. He looked at Zarina with great disappointment in his eyes.

"I'm so sorry. I'll help rebuild the Depot. I'll come in early. I'll stay late," Zarina told him.

"You were told not to tamper with pixie dust. I think it's best if you don't come in at all," Gary replied.

"What are you saying?" Zarina's eyes were moist with tears.

"You can no longer be a dust-keeper. It's simply too dangerous." Fairy Gary left Zarina and flew to the queen. "We'll start rebuilding in the morning."

Zarina was devastated. She turned to Tink and the rest of the girls, but they didn't know how to help.

Zarina's plans had gone wrong. All wrong. Tears streaming down her face, she turned around and ran away. She had never felt more alone.

An hour later, she'd packed up all her things, including her lab journal and the rest of her pixie dust. Then she coated her wings with golden pixie dust and left Pixie Hollow behind.

Chapter Three

One year later...

Iridessa, Rosetta, Vidia, and Silvermist were standing behind the stage curtain, ready for their act in Pixie Hollow's annual celebration.

"Welcome one, welcome all to the Four Seasons Festival! Tonight, talent from every season will gather together to celebrate all the realms of Pixie Hollow," the master of ceremonies announced.

Iridessa peeked out through a slit in the curtain and saw that the grandstands were full. "Wow! Can you believe it? Everyone in

Pixie Hollow is here."

"It's so great to have the winter fairies join us," Silvermist said, looking over Iridessa's shoulder.

Rosetta laughed. "I'll say it is." She tipped her head toward a handsome fairy in the winter frozen section. "It's enough to give you the vapors."

Tink was tinkering with the ornate music box that was part of the act. She was having trouble fixing a button.

"Tinker Bell, don't you tinkers ever stop tinkering?" Vidia asked.

"I can't seem to get this latch to open." Tink pushed the button over and over. Nothing happened.

WHAM! She smacked it with her fist.

KACHUNK! The panel popped open.

"Ugh. It had better not stick like that for our grand finale!" Tink said.

The sound of a loud horn made the girls turn around.

"Is it starting?" Tink asked Fawn.

"No," she replied. "That's just Clank."

In the stands, Clank was blowing an annoying horn. "Thing's pretty loud, eh, Bobble?!"

Bobble agreed. "Indeed, my bugling buddy."

"Sure makes me thirsty, though." Clank chugged a large drink.

Just then, the lights went down. The show began with a light snowfall all around the amphitheater.

"It's starting!" Clank shouted, full of excitement.

Several winter fairies skated out onto a sheet of ice. They all carried flowers.

From the royal box, Queen Clarion and the ministers watched while the crowd cheered.

Bobble whistled.

"Uh, Bobble?" Clank leaned toward his friend, indicating he needed to use the bathroom.

"Ohhh no. Already?" Bobble's eyes flitted

from Clank to the sign for the bathroom.

"Hold these." Clank dumped his horn and mug into Bobble's lap.

"But the show just started," Bobble protested.

"Ask them to wait!" Clank said as he rushed toward the exit.

Backstage, Tink looked over her friends' shoulders.

"Hi, Peri!" Tink waved. Peri waved back. Periwinkle was a frost fairy who Tink had discovered was her relative not too long ago.

"That's my sister!" Tink grinned, turning to talk to her friends.

Peri and her friends put frost on their flowers as the ice spectacular continued.

A lone fairy sneaked into the back of the theater, hiding in the shadows. She flew around the amphitheater, sprinkling pink pixie dust through the crowd. Red flower buds began to sprout and grow.

Silvermist saw the blossoms and asked Rosetta, "Ro, did you do those? That wasn't in rehearsal!"

"Wasn't me," Rosetta said. "I never work with poppies; the pollen makes me sleepy."

Tink noticed the mystery fairy far away. She had long, wild red hair. "Wait. Is that Zarina?"

"She's back?" Vidia asked.

"What's with that wild hair?" Rosetta said, noticing the way Zarina's bright red hair flowed down her back.

The winter fairies finished their performance. The crowd went crazy then, cheering even louder as they noticed the red flowers growing around the amphitheater.

"Ohh. Spring must be next! That's my favorite. I hope Clanky doesn't miss it!" Bobble looked back toward the bathroom sign. Clank was still outside.

"Oooh!" A shout rose from the audience

when the poppies popped open. Pollen began spraying everywhere.

"Oh, lovely! Oh—" Fairy Mary began.

Suddenly Rosetta started flitting around in a panic. "Guys. Guys! We gotta hide—now!" she shouted to Tinker Bell and the gang.

"Ro, what are you doing? What's wrong?" the girls all asked as Rosetta shoved them backward, away from the pollen.

When the pollen took effect, every fairy in the theater fell asleep.

Bobble blew a weak honk on Clank's horn before snoozing.

The queen, the ministers, and Fairy Mary all started snoring.

High above the amphitheater, Zarina smiled at what she'd done.

Clank came out of the bathroom and headed back toward the amphitheater. He saw Zarina fly by, but he was too excited to pay her any attention. He worked his way through the crowd, careful not to step on toes or wings. "'Scuse me—sorry—yes, me again—coming through—no, no, don't get up—sorry, shoulda flown—"

He took back his stuff from Bobble and plopped into his seat.

"Thank you, Bobble. What did I miss?"

When Clank noticed everyone around him—even Bobble—was asleep, he began blowing the horn, desperately trying to wake up the fairies.

Across Pixie Hollow, Zarina was at the Blue Pixie Dust Vault. She put in the code she'd memorized, and the Blue Dust storage chest popped open. She raised her head slightly when she heard Clank's horn blowing but ignored it. She reached for the precious dust....

Back at the amphitheater, Clank was flying frantically and shouting, "WAKE UP! WAKE UP!

PLEASE! ANYONE?!"

He listened and heard small voices from behind the stage curtain calling, "Help."

The girls were hiding in Tink's music box.

"Oh, oh! Miss Bell?" He tried to open the box.

"Clank, help! We're stuck!" Tink said.

"Right! How does it open?" It took a minute, but Clank found the latch.

"Push the button," Tink told him.

The door dropped, and the girls crawled out.

"Air!" Iridessa gasped.

"I could hardly breathe in that thing." Silvermist hugged Clank.

"Thank you, Clank," Vidia said.

"Yeah, thanks!" Fawn added.

Clank pointed back toward the audience. "You have got to see this."

The girls and Clank flew to the amphitheater. There were sleeping fairies everywhere.

"Huh?" Iridessa said as Silvermist gasped.

Fawn and Vidia were shocked.

"Are they...?" Clank whispered the question.

"No. Goodness, no. They are in a deep sleep," Rosetta said.

"For how long?" Fawn asked.

"At least a couple o' days," Rosetta said.

"Why would Zarina do this?" Vidia didn't understand why her friend would sprinkle sleeping dust on everyone.

Tink turned to Clank. "Did you see her?"

"No, no," he began, then said, "Yes! Yes! I saw her flying toward the Dust Depot!"

Tink's eyes grew wide. She gasped in horror.

A minute later, the girls were at the Blue Pixie Dust Vault.

It was empty.

"The Blue Pixie Dust." Silvermist was about to cry.

"Ohh, this is bad," Iridessa said.

"Uh, yeah," Vidia agreed.

Iridessa said, "Without it, the tree can't make pixie dust! And if the tree can't make pixie dust—" She was worried.

"We can't fly," Tink finished.

31

Iridessa started shaking. "Can't fly...can't fly... hooo...okay..."

Vidia patted her back. "Deep breaths. That's it. Deep breaths..."

Silvermist turned to Tink. "What could she want it for?"

"I don't know. But we have to get it back." Tink said to Clank, "Clank, stay here and watch over everyone."

"I'm on it!" He headed back to the amphitheater.

"Especially the winter fairies." Before flying away, Tink called to him, "Make sure they get a steady stream of snow."

"Right!" Clank promised he'd ride the bike-like snowmaker. Then repeated a little softer, "Right." He had a job to do.

Chapter Four

The girls zoomed through the woods.

"The Blue Dust has a strong glow. If we can just spot it..." Iridessa looked around. "There!"

They took off, flying at top speed.

"Whoa! She's movin' fast!" Vidia struggled to keep up.

The girls screamed when an owl startled them.

"Sorry!" Fawn apologized to the bird.

Fog filled the forest, making flying difficult. It was hard to see where they were going.

"Where is all this fog comin' from?" Rosetta asked.

Silvermist knew. "It's mist. We must be

getting near the coast."

Up ahead, the blue glow began to fade.

"We're losing her!" Tink worried.

"Over there!" Fawn pointed to the treetops.

When they got high enough to see, the girls were stunned at what they found.

Far below, anchored in the foggy cove, there was a ship.

"It's p-p-p—" Iridessa was so scared, she couldn't say the word.

So Tinker Bell said it instead. "Pirates!"

Out in the water, a rowboat was headed for the ship. A faint blue glow lit the boat.

"Great. Now there are pirates." Vidia shivered.

"Maybe they're nice pirates?" Silvermist suggested.

"Right." Vidia wasn't convinced.

"They must have captured her. Forced her to take the dust," Tink said.

Fawn flitted up and bravely pointed to the ship. "We have to rescue Zarina!"

"But, but...they're pppp—"

34

Iridessa still couldn't believe her eyes.

"Pirates. We know." Vidia groaned.

Two pirates were rowing the little boat. Port was short and peg-legged while Starboard was thin and lanky.

"Magnificent!" James, a cabin boy, exclaimed as they moved swiftly through the water.

"Fine haul!" Starboard said while straightening his kilt.

"We got their Blue Dust!" Port's belly wiggled as he chuckled.

"It's not theirs anymore!" Starboard cheered.

Port echoed, "It is theirs no longer!"

Starboard moaned. "I just said that, ya daft potato muncher!"

Port began to repeat himself again. Starboard rolled his eyes.

While the pirates argued, the fairies crept along the side of the boat. Tink peeked through a small knothole. All she could see were the boots of the men rowing and a blue glow.

"They're holding her in the bottom of the boat," Tink told the others.

Nearby, the men kept arguing.

"You've got a right wee brain, ya know that?" Starboard said.

"Still smart enough to know we got their dust," Port countered.

Iridessa held her fingers over her eyes, afraid to see the pirates.

Tink moved to another knothole closer to the front.

The fairies were all surprised by what they discovered: Zarina was there, dressed like a pirate.

"Let me just say your plan worked perfectly, Captain," James said with a small bow to Zarina.

Zarina lifted a sack of Blue Dust like a trophy.

Port and Starboard laughed.

The fairies pulled back; all six of them had eyes wide with shock.

"Captain?" Tink breathed the word.

"Here's to perfect plans," Port congratulated Zarina.

"Aye, perfect!" Starboard said.

Zarina laughed.

"I can't wait 'til the other lads hear!" Port bragged, nodding toward the large pirate ship in the distance.

"Guess she doesn't need rescuing," Vidia whispered to Tink.

Tink frowned.

Noting Zarina's adventurous outfit, Rosetta said, "But now the hair makes sense."

Iridessa turned to look at Tinker Bell. "What do we do now?"

"Let's just get the dust and get out of here," Tink said.

Port and Starboard continued rowing...and arguing.

"Aye, a little bit of pillage, a little bit of plunder," Port was saying when—OOF! Using her talent, Rosetta moved the oar to his head with seaweed.

Then she zipped around to Starboard's side and made seaweed grab his oar, too.

WHACK! Starboard held his hurting head.

Zarina flew into the air while James looked overboard. He saw Rosetta and Iridessa.

"Huh?! Fairies?!" James gasped.

Suddenly, a moonbeam shot into James's eyes. The bright light was reflected off the water by Iridessa's talent, blinding him. He winced.

Zarina gripped the dust sack, trying to get away, but Vidia blocked her.

"Get her!" Port shouted toward Vidia.

"Outta my way." Starboard reached for the fairy.

Silvermist used her talent to whip up a wave.

"Whoa-ahhh!" the pirates on the boat shrieked

as the water tossed the ship around.

James lost his balance and fell down, pinning Zarina against the boat with his arm.

"You sack of bones, get off...." Port shouted at Starboard, who was on top of him.

During the chaos, Vidia snatched the Blue Dust sack and tossed it to Tink, saying, "Got it. Here."

The girls took off across the cove as fast as they could fly, heading toward shore.

"Oh, she's gettin' away," Port cried.

"They took the Blue Dust!" James shrieked.

Zarina pried herself free of James's arm and sped off after them.

As the girls came to a waterfall, Zarina trapped them, blocking their way. "Give me back that dust!"

"Zarina, why are you doing this?" Tink asked as she tossed the dust satchel to Iridessa. The satchel was then tossed around from girl to girl, playing keep-away from Zarina.

"If you give it to me, I'll give you quarter,"

Zarina replied.

Silvermist threw the bag to Rosetta. "Quarter? I think we need all of it," she said.

"Quarter means mercy," Zarina retorted. She tried to grab the bag.

"This dust belongs to Pixie Hollow," Tink said, pulling it away.

Zarina narrowed her eyes. "You had your chance." She reached into her own bag—which held many different colors of pixie dust—and threw a fistful at the girls.

The girls were knocked down. Tink dropped the sack. Zarina grabbed it as the girls crashed backward, falling through the waterfall.

Grinning, Zarina flew back to her boat with the sack of Blue Dust.

"Wake up. Tink, wake up...." Silvermist gave Tink a shake.

"Ugh...what happened?" Tink sat up and rubbed her eyes.

"The last thing I remember was Zarina throwing that dust at us," Silvermist said.

Tinker Bell noticed that half of Silvermist's dress had turned purple. "Your dress..."

Silvermist looked down and said, "I know. Umm..." She pointed out that Tink's own dress was now partially blue.

Tink looked at the others and discovered that their clothes had changed as well. Rosetta was now wearing orange. Fawn was in yellow. Iridessa was dressed in pink. And Vidia's gown had gone green.

"Is everyone all right?" Tink asked, standing up.

"I guess so," Fawn said.

"I'm not! Look at my outfit! Orange is not my color," Rosetta grumbled.

"Listen, we have to get out of here and go after Zarina," Tink said, drawing attention back to what was important. The waterfall was like a wall of water, blocking their path. "Silvermist, can you part the—"

WHOOSH! A jet of water shot out like a fire

hose when Tink touched it with her hand.

The fairies yelled at Tink to shut it off.

"I didn't do anything! I just—" She touched it again. The water jet shot out again, smacking the fairies hard. "Ohhh."

"Tink, could you stop not doing anything?" Vidia asked, twisting water out of her dress.

"It's okay; I got this." Silvermist reached out toward the water and flapped her wings. She shot up and hit her head on the rock overhang and slammed back down to the ground.

"That's weird. Here, lemme help you." Fawn moved to Silvermist, but as she walked through a beam of light, she reflected it like a crystal—and blinded everyone.

To turn off the light, Fawn quickly moved back into the shadows.

Temporarily blinded, Iridessa stumbled back and put her hand on a tiny plant. As soon as she touched it, the plant turned into a thick, leafy shrub. "Argh!"

"What did you do?" Vidia asked.

Iridessa was stuck inside the plant leaves. "I don't know!"

"EW EW EW EW!" Rosetta interrupted everyone. They all turned.

She was completely covered in cute, smiling bugs and worms. They were climbing up her legs and crawling up her shoulders. "GET 'EM OFF GET 'EM OFF GET 'EM OFF!" A spider kissed her nose. "GET 'EM OFF!"

Fawn and Vidia began picking the bugs off Rosetta.

"Wait a minute. Do you realize what this means?" Tink questioned. She had just figured it out.

Silvermist thought she knew. "Oh my gosh. Zarina switched our heads!"

"No, she switched our talents," Tink explained while wringing water out of her dress. "I must be a water fairy now."

"Oh, so that's why your dress is blue." Silvermist understood.

"And I guess you're a fast-flying fairy!"

Fawn grabbed a sunbeam. "I'm a light fairy!" She accidentally pointed the light into her own eyes. "Ow."

Iridessa peeked out from the plant leaves. "Garden fairy."

"Looks like I'm an animal fairy now. Huh. Lucky me," Rosetta said with a moan. She picked one last baby bug out of her hair.

"No...it can't be...." Vidia was horrified by the pom-poms on her shoes.

Fawn laughed. "You're a—"

"Don't say it!" Vidia cut her off.

Fawn smiled.

Vidia said, "Tinker Bell! Take these things back right now!" She shook her shoes.

Tink plucked the pom-poms off Vidia's shoes and, laughing, put them on her own.

Fawn laughed and elbowed Vidia. "You're a tinker now."

Vidia wasn't happy with her new role.

"Guys, come on. We gotta get outta here," Tink told the others.

"Well, you're the water fairy," Vidia reminded her with a groan. "Part the waters."

Tink took a deep breath and tried, but nothing happened.

"Um...use both hands this time," Silvermist suggested.

Tink concentrated. This time, the waterfall lifted, like a spoon under a faucet.

"Well, you don't see that every day," Silvermist said.

"Mmf, you guys better hurry. I can't...hold it...." Tink was shaking with effort. It was hard to keep the water up.

Silvermist went first, but she was unsteady and bumped Tink. Tink lost control as the others passed.

The tame waterfall became a wild waterslide. It carried the other fairies down with it on a crazy wet ride. They screamed the whole way.

Iridessa landed in some flowers, which grew quickly around her. They were out of control.

Silvermist was the only one who wasn't wet.

She helped Iridessa climb onto a rock.

Rosetta was sitting on a large, cracked egg buried in the sand. A big eye looked up at her. "Whoa."

"Guys, I think I broke somethin'." It was a baby crocodile, just hatched. Rosetta backed away slowly. "Uh...nice...little...harmless...sharp-toothed...hungry...croco—"

The baby croc hugged her, full of love.

The other fairies gasped in fear, but not Fawn. She grinned. "It's okay! When babies are born, they imprint on the first thing they see."

The baby croc gave Rosetta a big, toothy kiss.

"Uh, guys, sorry to interrupt." Tink looked at the crocodile and Rosetta. "But the pirate ship is gone!"

Chapter Five

Silvermist took off, rocketing into the upper atmosphere. She wobbled until she got the hang of soaring so high.

"Sil. Fast flyer. Check it out!" Vidia cheered her on.

When she didn't come back right away, Iridessa started to worry. "Where is she?"

Just then, Silvermist appeared. Her flying was okay, but her landing needed practice.

"WHOOOOAAAA!" she screamed as she crashed near the others. She picked the leaves out of her hair and said, "You guys, I saw it up the coast! Let's go!"

The others didn't move.

Silvermist came back. "Oh, right, you can't fly. Wet wings."

Vidia nodded. "Still, there's gotta be a way." She noticed Rosetta, who was being lovingly petted by the baby croc.

"'Scuse me, Ro—" Vidia inspected the croc's eggshell. "Hmmmm. Structurally sound enough. Strength-to-weight ratio seems good. If I had some rope..."

"You're thinking like a tinker," Fawn teased.

Vidia grumbled, then accepted her new talent. "Okay, fine. Get me some vines."

"Not a problem." Iridessa jumped off the rock and started walking. Vines grew around her feet until she was covered. "Will these do?" she muttered as the vines crawled over her head.

Vidia connected the vines to the eggshell. Silvermist tied the end around her waist and fluttered up. The girls piled into the little egg-boat they'd made. Vidia held the vines tight, like horse reins.

"Okay. Ready," Silvermist said.

"Wait for me!" Rosetta had to shake off the baby croc to get herself in the boat. The croc was sad about being left behind and refused to let go of Rosetta's leg. Rosetta shook him off, saying, "Gotta go," and climbed into the shell with the others.

Silvermist zoomed off with the egg-boat skipping across the waves behind her like a water-skiing inner tube.

"WHOAA—WHOAA—WHOAA!" the girls shrieked as the shell skipped across the water.

Fawn looked out. "There's the pirate ship!"

They were nearly there when cracks formed in the shell.

"You can slow down now!" Rosetta screamed while scooping water from their makeshift boat.

"Easy for you to say!" Silvermist struggled with her speed. A big wave was ahead of them. "Hold on!"

WHOMP! They hit the wave. The fairies were thrown from the shell just before it broke apart.

"AHHHHHHHHH!" everyone screamed.

KATHOONK! They landed in the barrel of one of the on-deck cannons.

As they untangled themselves and checked for bruises, the girls could hear the pirates laughing in another part of the ship.

"Well, at least our wings are dry now," Rosetta said.

"Yeah," Vidia groaned.

They heard a pirate named Yang announce, "Twenty-one-gun salute to the captain!"

"Right!" a pirate named Oppenheimer replied. "Twenty-one!"

The fairies looked at one another. This was not good.

"Nice boom," they heard a third voice say. His name was Bonito.

BOOM!

A cannon went off. Then another. The boat was shaking. One by one, the pirates were getting closer to firing the fairies' cannon.

They had to get out!

"I love it!" Bonito cheered.

"Ha-haaa! Music to my ears!" Oppenheimer agreed.

With their wings finally dry, the girls flew out of the cannon an instant before it fired. They landed on the yardarm and quickly hid behind some sails and ropes.

The pirates continued to enjoy firing the cannons. Their laughter echoed through the ship.

Suddenly Yang shouted, "Cease fire!"

Oppenheimer looked at him. Yang was steering the vessel. "What? What for? That was only seven," Oppenheimer said.

With a menacing growl, Yang waved two swords and snarled, "I say that was twenty-one."

"Right, ha ha ha!" Oppenheimer blew out the candle he was using to light fuses and stepped back. Yang was clearly in charge. "Twenty-one. Officially on the metric system, which is fine."

Tink fluttered out of hiding, and sneaking off, she motioned for the girls to follow. She whispered to the others, "C'mon, we've got to find that dust."

Below them, James was carrying a tray with six mugs of grog across the deck. "If I may, good sirs—I believe the proper acknowledgment would be a toast."

The pirates gathered around for drinks.

"Now, there is a good cabin boy," Oppenheimer said about James.

"A beautiful suggestion," said Bonito. He flopped down very, very close to the fairies. They moved just in time.

"Quite right. I could do with a bevvy!" Port put in.

"Quite thirsty meself," Starboard agreed.

James stopped a moment and looked up. Zarina was on deck. "If it pleases the captain?" He held out the tray toward her for permission to continue serving.

She nodded and jingled in fairy-speak, "You can tell those scurvy scallywags that it pleases the captain very much." James was clearly able to understand her.

"What'd she say?" Oppenheimer asked James.

"It does!" James loosely paraphrased her fairy-speak, holding up a pint glass.

The pirates swarmed James, grabbing mugs, leaving one tiny teacup alone on the tray.

"What could be more tasty?" Bonito asked.

"Two mugs!" Yang chuckled.

"He's got you there," Starboard agreed.

As the pirates carried on with their party, the girls followed James. "Your tea, Captain. Earl Grey, hot." She took the cup.

The pirates toasted her. "To our cunning captain."

Rosetta looked at Zarina and whispered to Tink, "Okay, you gotta love the boots."

James then said loudly, "Just one year ago, we'd lost everything, our ship turned adrift, and then we found her."

Zarina jingled, and James translated.

"Exactly. We needed a captain, and we humbly asked if she could make us fly."

"She didn't stop there!" Starboard said.

"No! She did one better, she did!" Port put in.

"Better indeed! Soon, she's gonna make the whole ship fly!" Oppenheimer was very excited.

"To flying!" The pirates clinked their cups.

"Fly?!" Tink mouthed the word to the others.

The pirates began to dance and sing about how great their lives would be once they could fly out of Never Land and plunder everywhere across the globe. Toward the end of the song, both Zarina and James had climbed to the very top of the mast. She looked out, then spun down, back to the deck, just as a shadow passed over the ship.

The pirates stopped dancing; Skull Rock loomed on the horizon.

They were almost there.

Chapter Six

In the dark cave with openings that looked like big hollow eyes, a nose, and a mouth, there was a massive tree. Ladders and scaffolding surrounded it.

"Oh," Tink gasped.

Iridessa said, "It looks like..."

"The Pixie Dust Tree back home," Rosetta finished the thought.

"Zarina must have grown it," Silvermist told them.

"So that's how they're gonna fly. She's gonna make pixie dust." Tink figured out the plan.

This was bad. Very, very bad.

"Ahoy, you biscuit-eating bilge rats!" Zarina said.

James translated her order for the crew. "Prepare to dock starboard!"

Zarina jingled her commands. James said, "Captain says, 'Raise the sails and step lively!'"

Port, Starboard, and Bonito heaved the heavy sails.

"Bring her around, Mr. Yang," James said.

"Bringing her around," Yang replied.

At the helm, Yang turned the ship's wheel. But he wasn't going fast enough for Zarina. She took over, spinning the wheel and perfectly parking the ship at the dock.

"Let go anchor! Get out all lines!" James shouted.

Port and Starboard did their jobs with gusto.

The gangplank was lowered. Several of the pirates went ashore.

James told the men, "Captain says, 'Restock

the ship! We set sail at dawn!'"

Yang replied, "Yes, Captain, load the ship. Right away."

The fairies watched Zarina leave her men to work. They followed her when she went inside the ship and through a fairy-sized door in the bigger door to the captain's quarters.

"Come on," Tink told the girls.

The fairies sneaked to the door, but it was locked. They had to hide when Starboard approached. They ducked behind a barrel only to find a rat in their hiding place. It hissed at them.

Fawn told Rosetta to get rid of it. "Animal fairy? You're up."

Rosetta boldly said to the rat, "Excuse me, mouse? Mr. Mouse? Would you mind terribly movin' on? We need this space to do a little hiding. Much obliged. Bye-bye."

The rat left.

"What a cute little mouse." Rosetta smiled. She'd done a good job.

"It was a rat," Fawn corrected.

"Ewww." Rosetta wrinkled her nose.

The rat went from the hiding place, straight to James.

"Hey, shoo, rat!" he said. It wouldn't go away and kept squeaking.

James went to the cabin door and knocked for Zarina. "Permission to enter, Captain?"

"This is our chance!" Tink was ready.

When James opened the door, she hurried forward. "Now!" The others followed, but only Tink, Silvermist, and Vidia made it inside. The door shut, leaving Iridessa, Fawn, and Rosetta outside.

Zarina's personal cabin was fitted with everything a fairy pirate captain might need, including a fancy laboratory. Compared to her house in Pixie Hollow, this was a mansion. She moved around the room, gathering the equipment she needed to sift and purify the Blue Dust.

Tink saw the bag of dust sitting nearby as James set a tray of berries and tiny cakes on the desk. "I had Oppenheimer make you your favorites," James said. He unloaded the treats and leaned the tray against the wall. "I know how much you like a little something sweet while you work."

Zarina jingled her thanks.

James said, "Well, you're quite welcome."

Zarina jingled instructions for James to follow. "I'll be needing the sifter next."

"Oh, yes, of course. Sorry." James looked through one drawer, then found it in another. He helped Zarina shake flakes of Blue Pixie Dust into a clear glass vial. "Look at that. It sparkles like a thousand sapphires." He smiled. "Ah, you're quite the little genius."

The girls sneaked behind the food tray.

Zarina jingled, and James replied, "It's hard to believe the other fairies didn't appreciate your talent." He added, "You know, I remember when I couldn't understand a single jingle."

Behind the tray, Silvermist moaned.

Vidia said, "She looks seasick...."

"This never happened when I was a water fairy," Silvermist said as she stumbled against the food tray.

"Oh no!" Vidia groaned.

CLANG! The food tray hit the floor.

James snapped around. He just missed seeing the girls, who were now hidden down by his foot. He set the tray upright again, going back to work with Zarina.

Silvermist gave the others a weak smile and whispered, "I'm fine."

On the other side of the door, Rosetta and Iridessa listened. Rosetta leaned away. She smelled something burning.

Behind Rosetta, Fawn was messing around with her talent, using light beams to burn smiley faces into a barrel.

"FAWN!" Rosetta whisper-yelled.

Startled, Fawn spun around. Her friends had to duck away from the hot light beams that nearly burned them.

"Oh, sorry," she said, shutting off the light.

"What're you doing?!" Rosetta demanded.

"What Dess does," Fawn replied.

Iridessa looked at the burn marks in the barrel. "That's not what I do."

"Well, stop it!" Rosetta warned.

"You shouldn't take light so lightly," Iridessa told Fawn.

Rosetta leaned back toward the door. Iridessa noticed that when Fawn had accidentally shot the fiery light, she'd cut off part of Rosetta's hair. It was smoky at the ends.

Iridessa turned to Fawn, wide-eyed.

"What?" Rosetta wanted to know what they were looking at.

Iridessa smiled. "What? No-nothin'. Nothin'. Nope."

Back in the cabin, Zarina held a tiny crystal bottle of Blue Dust.

"It's still so hard to believe this 'Blue Dust' can make 'Flying Dust.'" James was awed.

The girls were now in a drawer of the desk, listening and trying to come up with a plan.

James said to Zarina, "Ahh, so the secret is the infusion of the Blue Dust directly into the tree. I knew there was a method to your madness." He got up and went to look at the tree through the window.

Careful not to be seen, Vidia tried to snag the vial with a hastily tinkered fishhook-grapple. She directed the others, "Sil, you okay? Start throwing out the line."

Silvermist helped, though she was still seasick.

"Tink, open the drawer. As much as you can," Vidia said.

"Got it." She jumped to the task.

The girls heard James say, "So once the golden dust has been produced, the sluice will coat the ship with the perfect amount. At that point, we take to the skies!"

Zarina jingled happily.

Vidia was ready to stop their plan. "Sil," she whispered. "Hold the line." She reached out with the hook.

"No pirate I know could've imagined such a scheme," James complimented Zarina just as Vidia nabbed the vial.

It was hard work. With a grunt, Vidia accidentally dropped her fishhook-grapple.

The girls had to hide.

Zarina picked up the bottle of purified Blue Dust, and James handed her a sword.

"You've turned out to be quite the pint-sized prodigy, if I may say," James told Zarina.

Zarina flipped the blade in the air and then sheathed it.

When James closed the drawer, he didn't realize he locked the fairies inside. He and Zarina left the room.

Rosetta, Iridessa, and Fawn were able to fly in before the door closed. They found the others in the drawer.

"Y'all okay?" Rosetta asked.

Tinker Bell answered, "Yeah. They're headed for the tree. C'mon!"

Vidia saw Rosetta's hair from behind. "Whoa. What is up with your ha—"

Iridessa interrupted. "Heeeeey, hey, we should—we should catch up with Tink!" She put a finger over her mouth and warned Vidia, "SHHHH!" Rosetta would go nuts if she knew. Better to keep it a secret as long as possible.

They flew out of the cabin and around the side of the ship to find the pirates working on the scaffolding around the tree.

James was in charge. "Right, watch the angle of the flume. Too much pitch and she'll overflow. Make sure the seams are sealed. Captain doesn't want to lose a single grain of that precious dust."

After making sure no one was watching, the fairies fled to the top of the Pixie Dust Tree. But

Iridessa got too close, and new branches began to grow. "Sorry!" she told the others. "I barely touched it."

"Don't touch it at all," Tink warned her.

"Just hover," Vidia advised.

"Yeah...hover," Rosetta echoed.

"Yeah, all right. All right," Iridessa said, watching her wings.

Below them, Zarina landed next to a pixie dust well, much like the one at the Pixie Dust Tree back home. She had the Blue Dust bottle in her hands.

"As soon as she's gone, we'll grab the dust vial and get out of here," Vidia said.

"Maybe we should try to talk to her," Tink said.

"Yeah, 'cause that worked out so well back at the waterfall," Vidia replied.

Tink sighed.

A bee buzzed up to Iridessa and examined the flower in her hair. "Hey, shoo," she told it. But the bee wouldn't leave. "Heeey!

Hey, heeey! GO, GO, GO!"

Distracted by the pesky bee, Iridessa accidentally leaned on a branch.

SCRUUUNCH! It started to grow!

In her panic, Dess grabbed it, but that just made it grow more. "No! Stop growing. Stop growing please, branch. No...OH NOOO!"

The branch shot out, taking the girls for a ride along with it.

"AHHHHH!" the fairies screamed, and just as Zarina was about to overturn the Blue Dust bottle into the tree's well, she saw the girls hanging over her head.

Zarina pulled out her sword, ready to fight for the Blue Dust.

Fawn pretended that the branch thing was their plan all along. "Ha! We gotcha!"

"Did you really think by switching our talents you could beat us?" Rosetta asked Zarina.

"Looks that way," Zarina said, and then whistled. Within moments, the pirates swooped in, swinging on ropes from the scaffolding. They had swords and fishnets. The girls didn't have a chance. They were immediately captured.

"Got 'em! Well done! Got 'em all in one swell foop, I did!" Oppenheimer said, waving a spatula.

The pirates growled menacingly.

"Zarina, don't do this! Come back home." Tink was going to try to talk to her.

"I'll never go back to Pixie Hollow," Zarina replied.

"You don't belong here," Tinker Bell said.

Zarina thought for a moment, then said, "This is exactly where I belong, Tink."

James added, "We appreciate what she can do. Treasure it, actually." He pointed to Oppenheimer, who was holding the girls wrapped in the netting.

"Put them below. And keep your eye on them," Yang instructed Oppenheimer.

The girls struggled to get free, but they were trapped.

Zarina looked away as they were carried off.

"Captain? Are you all right?" James asked,

noticing her frown.

Zarina raised her arm and jingled.

"Captain says, 'Back to work, gentlemen,'" James told the others.

Chapter Seven

Oppenheimer carried the girls below to the gun deck, which was also the kitchen galley. Cannonballs and cantaloupes lined the walls, along with shelves of stolen china and silver.

He dumped them into a wooden crab cage, then slammed the top and locked it.

"Welcome to your new cabin!" he laughed.

Tink rattled the cage. She was angry.

Oppenheimer grinned. "Oh my. Oh no, no, no. You won't be getting out of there." A tiny alarm clock rang, and he returned to his job as chef. "Oh! Me stock is ready!" He went to a boiling pot and, using tongs, pulled out an ugly, sharp-toothed fish skeleton. Above his head was an odd portrait of an old pirate lady in a chef's hat. He told the picture, "Oh, look at the lovely. Oh, lovely. That is good eatin' right there. Isn't it, Mum?" He answered his own question in a higher lady's voice. "Yes, it is, darling."

While Tink continued to rattle the cage, he talked to himself. "Oh, let me see...what shall I make tonight? Well, I've still got some lard and some old cabbage." The chef gathered supplies.

"We need a plan," Rosetta said, desperately looking around the kitchen to see what they could do.

Out at the Pixie Dust Tree, Zarina plugged the Blue Dust bottle into the well and watched as the tree began to shake. Slowly, a small trickle of golden pixie dust seeped out, like sap.

The pirates celebrated with clanking swords and cheers.

James announced with pure joy, "We're going to fly!"

Zarina smiled bigger than she ever had before. "To flying."

The fairies stared out of the crab cage, watching Oppenheimer peel potatoes.

"Cold gruel," he muttered. "With a little bit of sawdust. Dash of rodent, sautéed of course. Some carrots? No."

One of the potatoes slipped away from him and rolled down the floor. "Hey, where you think you're goin', little fella? Ha-ha!"

The instant he went after it, Rosetta said, "Now's our chance. Go, go, go, go." The girls put their legs out of the bottom slats of the cage and, by holding the bars and working together, managed to move across the room.

"Well, that's all right. There's a three-day rule on this...isn't it?" Oppenheimer asked himself.

"Come on, all together," Rosetta said. "Not that way. This way!"

Tink tried to help. "To the left! Now!"

"I'm going as fast as I can," Iridessa said.

Oppenheimer noticed and stopped them. "Oh, not today, my darlings. Would you be kind enough to hold this for me?" He raised the cage onto a high table, then plopped a giant sack of potatoes on top of it, trapping them in place. "Perfect."

Vidia frowned. "Anybody else got an idea?"

Zarina watched golden dust come from the tree, funneling into a barrel.

"Absolutely astonishing. Just imagine, flying like a bird." James looked at Zarina. "Hmf. Of course, you do that all the time. What's it like? How do you even steer?"

"It's pretty simple, actually. Lean left," she said in a jingle. "Lean right, fly right!"

James didn't seem to understand, so Zarina took a handful of dust from the golden stream and led James to the edge of a platform overlooking the pirate cove below.

"Whoa. Uugh...uhh, he-he...uh...this is... uhh, wha?" James shivered, concerned about the height.

Zarina grinned. "Are you afraid?"

James crossed his arms and tried to look brave. "Afraid? Lead on, Captain!"

Zarina sprinkled him with the pixie dust. He floated into the air.

"I'm, I'm doing it! I'm fly—" James was saying while Zarina led him off the platform. She let go of his hand. "YYYYYYING!" He plunged toward the water below!

Zarina dived after him, but on his own he pulled up just in time. His course cut through the pirates, sending them scattering for cover.

"Look out, mates!" James circled around the cave, flapping his arms and legs. "Whoa-whoa-whoaaaaa!" He was out of control.

Zarina flew next to him, laughing.

"What's so funny?!" he asked.

"You can't fly like that! Put your legs together," she instructed.

James followed and started to get the hang of it. "WA-HOOOO!"

Zarina landed on his head, like riding in the bow of the ship. She pointed forward, saying, "Bring us home."

"Aye, aye, Captain!" James swooped past the masts to the ship. The pirates all cheered.

Zarina and James landed next to the ship's helm. Zarina hopped onto the steering wheel.

"It works! It really works!" James was very excited. "Soon, we'll have enough dust to make the whole ship fly, right, Zarina?" She smiled. "As long as we have the Blue Dust, we'll never run out of flying dust. Right again?"

"Right again, James," Zarina confirmed.

Suddenly, James's eyes grew dark. He chuckled. "Well, then...we won't need you anymore." He grabbed Zarina in his fist. Yang pulled a lamp from behind his back, and James tossed Zarina inside. Yang slammed it shut.

Zarina was stunned. She trembled in fear.

James told the pirates, "Our plan worked

perfectly!" Then to Zarina, he said, "Fairies are such gullible creatures." A school ring on his hand glimmered. "Aren't they, lads? No match for an Eton education such as mine." He waved the lamp with Zarina inside.

Yang raised his eyebrows. "What?!"

Starboard laughed. "He's a smart one, isn't he?!"

James announced, "The power of the pixie dust is finally ours."

The pirates laughed and celebrated.

"We've had enough kissing up to that pint-sized prima donna!" Yang said.

"No quarter for her," Port announced.

Oppenheimer suggested she be forced to walk the plank. The others agreed.

"Let's make her walk a tiny little plank!" Bonito said.

"Right, little plank!" Port added.

James sneered. "She can fly, you cretins."

"Oh, right." The pirates realized their mistake. One of them was slower than the others. It took a minute, then the pirate said, "She'd just fly away. I get it."

Bonito tossed a sword in a scabbard to James. "Mi capitan!"

James caught it and was happy to have his weapon.

"What if we tie her wings together?" Port asked.

James shook his head and began making plans. "There's no stopping us now. We'll plunder every port in all the seven seas!" He called to his crew. "Prepare to get under way, you scurvy scallywags! We've got a ship to fly!"

While the pirates got ready, James laughed at Zarina, saying, "As for you, you'll make a fine little night-light."

He took Zarina to *his* cabin. James set the lamp on the table, took out proper captain's clothing, and dropped into his real accent. "Swoggle me eyes. Now there's a sight." Seeing Zarina's sad and sorry face, he told her, "Oh, don't feel foolish. I was just too clever for you, that's all." He pulled out a book from a shelf and removed a secret key. The key opened a chest with maps inside. James put one map on the table; it showed the way from Skull Rock to the second star.

Zarina couldn't believe her eyes. She'd put the world in jeopardy.

"Ahhh yeees, now you see, my little fairy, navigating the Never Seas is one thing, but to chart a course for the sky...not only do you need longitude and latitude, but you also need altitude!"

He continued to chart the way to the second star.

Zarina struggled to get the lamp door open.

James flashed her a look. "Ah, now, let's not be a sore loser." He stabbed a knife in that map, then opened another, bigger map—a map of the world.

"Ha ha haaaa! Once we're past the second star...the world will be my oyster! And I don't even like oysters." He laughed. "We'll be in and out of every port so fast they won't even know what hit them."

Zarina threw herself at the locked door, desperate to get out. The lamp tipped and fell. James set it up again, saying, "No. Nice try, but it's fairy-proof. Brilliant, right?"

Oppenheimer's cooking alarm clock echoed through the floorboards, interrupting his planning. James stomped his feet and bellowed, "Oppenheimer! That ticking's driving me mad!"

In the kitchen, Oppenheimer heard the boss's shout. "Right!" he called out. Then muttered, "It's just a clock, you know!" To his mother's portrait, he said, "Well, not to worry, pretty soon we'll be flying so high it'll make these high seas look downright low!"

Trapped in their cage, the girls were frazzled and frustrated.

"Crazy!" Iridessa looked at the chef.

"Like we have a choice!" Vidia said.

Fawn grunted. "Ugh!"

Silvermist tried to keep them all calm. "C'mon, guys, we'll get out of this."

Rosetta was impatient and crabby. "Well, we wouldn't even be in it if our new garden fairy didn't grow branches willy-nilly."

"You're not saying this is my fault." Iridessa was crabby, too.

"Hmm...if the flower fits," Rosetta said, glaring at her.

Across the room, Oppenheimer was working, but the arguing in the cage was upsetting him. "How can I cook with all that infernal jingle-janglin'? There's only one thing to do." He waved his knife at the girls. Then...WHACK! He cut off the ends of two carrots and stuffed them in his ears as plugs. "Oh, much better, don't you think, Mum?" Oppenheimer asked the painting.

He couldn't hear them anymore, but the fairies kept arguing.

"None of it would've happened if you would

have come over to help me with the bee!" Iridessa stared at Rosetta.

"Are you saying this is my fault?" Rosetta asked.

"Well, if the rose fits," Iridessa grunted.

"Let's not point fingers," Vidia started, then changed her mind and declared, "It's Zarina's fault!"

Silvermist suddenly noticed the baby croc appear in a nearby cannon hole. "Guys?"

"Right! What about her?!" Fawn didn't see the croc yet.

Silvermist got between them and pointed. "Guys...Look!"

The girls both turned to find the croc's nose sniffing through the cannon hole.

"Oh, great. Just what I need," Rosetta muttered. To the croc, she scolded, "Ah ah ah. Bad crocodile. Baaaad croc. I am not your mother!"

She was about to send him away when Tink said, "Wait. Rosetta, he can get us out of here."

"You're right." Rosetta changed her attitude, saying, "Good. Good crocodile. Come here. Come here, crocky. Come to Mama. Good crocky! Goooood crocky!"

Croc hopped into the galley. He stood up on his hind legs and began to pull on a tablecloth underneath the crate. The crate started to slide.

"Okay, now pull us off the table! Come here! Come to Mama, that's right, sugar!" Rosetta said in a sweet voice.

He gave it one last big tug, and the crate fell off the table.

CRASH!

"Just what is going on here?" Oppenheimer raised his head and took out the earplugs. The crate was destroyed, and the fairies were getting away. The croc started at him.

"A stowaway, is it?" He tried to grab the fairies, but they were too fast. "Oh, uh...you little...oh no...you don't!"

"Go! Hurry!" Tink told the others.

As Rosetta and Iridessa raced past, Oppenheimer

clapped a pot and lid together, trapping Rosetta.

"Ha! Gotcha!" Oppenheimer said.

"Rosetta!" the girls shouted.

The croc wasn't going to let Oppenheimer mess with Rosetta. He chomped down on the chef's butt. Oppenheimer flew straight up in the air, smacking into an overhanging pan, and fell to the ground, out cold.

Rosetta ran free and hugged the baby croc tight. "Oh, good job, crocky. You are such a good little boy! Yes you are! What a good little widdle snuggle wuggums." She kissed him on his nose.

"That's his mama," Silvermist said with a tear in her eye.

"Okay, enough." Vidia called them to action. "Let's get outta here."

Tink blocked the way. "Wait. We can't just race out. They'll see us."

"Hmmm." Vidia began to think of a way....

Chapter Eight

The men were loading barrels full of supplies onto the boat.

"Make ready to sail!" James ordered.

"Aye, aye, Captain," Yang said.

"Aye, aye." Starboard gave a salute.

Port dropped the gangplank down and headed to the dock.

Starboard said, "Move it, Port."

"I'll move it in my own good time," Port replied.

Bonito was carrying a large crate when he spotted a rat. "I love the life of a pirate," he said, "but I hate rats."

He passed the galley, not noticing anything

strange as the door opened and a wobbly pirate walked out.

Tink floated in the air, holding up the hat. Vidia was keeping the pirate coat below it aloft. "See anything?" Vidia asked.

"Nope. All clear up here!" Tink reported.

"Well, it's not clear down here! It stinks!" Rosetta complained from inside one pirate shoe. Fawn was in the other one.

"I know, isn't it great? Smells just like skunk," Fawn said.

Rosetta chuckled. "Spoken like a true animal fairy."

"I wish." Fawn wanted her own power back.

Vidia told them how to move. "All right, you guys. Remember, right arm, left foot. Got it?"

They said they knew, but they didn't really.

"Sil, I'm right and you're left," Iridessa told Silvermist. They were in charge of the arms.

"Right!" Silvermist said.

"No, left!" Iridessa replied.

"I mean, left!" Silvermist thought she was

clear. "And you're right!"

Vidia shook her fairy head. "Let's go."

Silvermist replied, "Aye, aye."

They walked straight ahead and smacked into the mast pole.

"Big pole," Silvermist said while everyone rubbed their bruises.

Vidia started over. "Back back back back back back. Forward forward forward." Finally, the shoes met up with the body, and the hat was over the coat.

The girls made it down the gangplank.

"Hey, you swabs, work faster!" Yang called out to the fairy pirate, thinking it was the chef. "Oppenheimer, don't forget the kippers."

The pirate's arm moved in an awkward salute.

The fairy pirate passed Starboard, who was carrying a heavy load of a barrel and a lot of rope. Starboard playfully grabbed the coat arm and swung the pirate around for a happy dance. "We're gonna fly, mates! We're gonna fly!"

"It's a do-si-do," Rosetta said as they were spun around.

"I can't dance," Fawn warned.

The girls were getting dizzy, when suddenly Port came toward them. He also had a heavy load. It was piled so high, he could barely see.

Vidia warned the girls, "Uh-oh. Look out."

"Whoa. Would you watch where I'm goin'?" Port said just before he accidentally hooked the coat's other sleeve. The hat and shoes were pulled away with Starboard while the coat went the other direction with Port.

"Fly!" Vidia shouted as they were revealed.

Tink, Vidia, Silvermist, and Iridessa headed for the tree. Rosetta and Fawn ran awkwardly behind them in the shoes.

"Come on!" Vidia called to them.

The fairies flitted up into the branches before they gathered at the well where the Blue Pixie Dust vial was releasing precious flakes. Silvermist took the vial out of the well and put a cap on it. She handed the vial to Tink.

The tree stopped making golden dust.

"We got it!" Tink said. The girls flew away as fast as they could.

"RETURN THAT BLUE DUST!" James shouted.

Something terrible in his voice made the girls stop and look back. James was standing on a high platform, dangling the lamp holding Zarina over the water.

"Or your friend is done for," he warned. "That's right. *Captain* Zarina has been relieved of duty." He sneered.

Tink was clutching the vial of Blue Dust tightly.

"No, Tink!" Zarina protested sadly.

But Tink made a decision; she flew back to the tree and put the dust back in the well. The golden pixie dust began to flow again.

"You truly are a talented fairy." James grinned before giving a signal to his men. A long pipe was attached to the tree. It swung past the fairies to a spot over the high crow's nest at the top of the biggest mast. With a flick of a lever, the gold dust began to sprinkle down over the ship.

"Prepare to cast off!" James told his crew. "Weigh anchor and get ready to fly, me hearties!"

"Casting off," Starboard called out.

The ship began to rise. Yang took the helm.

Just coming out onto the deck, Oppenheimer looked up toward the sky. "It's working! I can't believe my eye."

"Weigh anchor," Yang echoed James's command.

The pirates were thrilled that they were flying.

As the ship rose past the Pixie Dust Tree, James grabbed the remaining Blue Pixie Dust, then jumped back on board. He was going to need every last speck. He'd save what was left for a time in the future when they wanted to make more golden dust.

James sneered at Zarina in the lamp. "Bon voyage, little captain." Without another thought, he tossed her into the sea.

As the lamp sank beneath the surface, Tink and the girls dived toward the water.

Tink pushed the water down so that Vidia could grab the top of Zarina's lamp.

"Come on!" Vidia said as her hands became wet and slick. The girls had created a chain so that none of them would get pulled into the deep sea.

It took great strength, but finally, they pulled the lamp to the surface. As the lamp filled with water, the girls kicked at the small door latch.

"Help, please! Help!" Zarina cried.

The door opened just in time. The lamp sank to the ocean floor, but Zarina was safe.

The girls escaped together to the rocks, near the scaffolding of the tree.

"Here, I'll dry you off," Silvermist told Zarina. She created a wind.

In the distance, the girls could see the ship rising high into the sky, headed toward the second star. They sighed.

"Are you okay?" Tink asked Zarina.

"You saved me....Why?" Zarina asked.

"Let's just say...we're offering you quarter," Tink said.

"I'm so sorry." A small tear rolled down Zarina's face.

Tink smiled softly.

Zarina wiped the tear away. "I think we can still get the dust back. But we have to do it before they pass the second star; otherwise we'll never find them. They'll be gone forever." She stood, ready to go and fight.

"Then let's stop them before they get there." Vidia stepped next to her.

With Zarina as the captain, leading the fairies, they all took off.

They had to stop that ship.

James was at the wheel. His ship rose higher and higher into the sky. "We need more altitude. Port,

Starboard, get up the mizzen and raise the royal!"

"Aye, aye, Captain! Raisin' the royal!" Port and Starboard said together. They climbed up the mizzenmast. The sails unfurled, and the wind moved the ship faster and higher.

"More pixie dust!" James pulled a lever, and more golden dust rained down over the boat from the crow's nest.

As the girls reached the ship, they heard James ask the pirates, "Who's in the mood to plunder?"

Zarina turned to the fairies. "You guys turn the ship around. I'm getting back the Blue Dust." She kicked in a window to the captain's cabin, and they all went in.

"Right," Tink agreed.

James navigated the ship around a cloud, and suddenly, he could see their goal. "Look alive, men! The second star! Dead ahead. Nothing but smooth sailing!"

WHAM!

The captain's door fell off its broken hinges and slammed to the deck. There were the fairies, now dressed in pirate outfits.

Port and Starboard were perplexed as they started shouting, "Fairies! Fairies! It's the fairies!"

James looked down from the bridge. "She's back? Well, get them off my ship."

"Gladly," Yang said.

The pirates rushed forward, drawing their weapons.

The fight began. The girls jabbed pirates with their swords, which were actually hatpins.

"You call that a jab?" Yang asked.

The pirates chuckled.

Starboard faked pain when Silvermist attacked him. "Oh, the pain. The agony." He chuckled. "Just kidding."

Rosetta was fighting Port, but he was laughing. "Oh, she's deadly, this one. Oh, you got me! Ha-ha. I didn't feel a thing! Maybe the other side." Rosetta tried harder. "Whoa. She's mad. Who's the mad little girl?"

Rosetta was wearing an eye patch. It was hindering her ability to see, so she lifted it and went after him again.

"It's actually quite amusing," James said from the bridge, where he kept the boat on course. "Stand your ground, men!" he called, laughing loudly.

Out of nowhere, Zarina rocketed at James. She hit the strap around his neck that held the vial of Blue Dust. The leather strap tore, just a little.

She held up her sword in a fencing pose.

"Yang! The helm!" James called over his shoulder.

Yang had Tink's and Vidia's swords in his grasp, but let them go to help his captain. "Aye, aye, Captain. Ladies...until we meet again." With a bow, he bid them farewell.

"Great," Vidia said, noting that Yang had bent both their swords.

"You dare to fight the captain, do you?" James challenged Zarina, ready to fence.

"Only until I get that dust," Zarina said.

"Well, this should be fun." James laughed.

Yang took over the wheel while James faced Zarina.

Zarina charged. James easily moved out of her blade's path and barely missed her with his own sword.

Below them, on the main deck, Bonito was swishing a net at Fawn and Iridessa, as if they were pesky flies.

"Okay, this isn't working," Fawn told Iridessa.

Just then, Iridessa caught the sun in her eyes. It gave her an idea. "Fawn, the spyglass!"

"Brilliant!" Fawn knew what she meant.

Fawn darted up to the spyglass in the crow's nest. There, she bent the last light of day through the telescope—shooting scorching light beams down at Bonito.

He pulled out his sword. "Ha. You tiny thing!"

He went after Iridessa, but Fawn's light beam hit him in the eyes, temporarily blinding him and causing him to flip over the railing. He landed in the water with a splash.

"Uh, man overboard?" Yang questioned, surprised.

"I did it!" Fawn cheered.

"That's it!" Vidia said.

WHACK! The girls jammed their swords into the wood floor. They didn't need them anymore.

"Our talents!" Tink was clear how they could win.

"Stop them, you imbeciles. They're six-inch fairies," James scolded his crew.

When the pirates came after them, the girls scattered.

They were ready to take down the ship.

Chapter Nine

Vidia zipped over to the wheel, shouting, "Fawn!"

Fawn turned the spyglass, zapping Yang several times with bright light. In a flash, Vidia kicked the steering wheel, spinning it around in fast circles. "Sil! Whirlwind!"

Silvermist quickly whipped up a whirlwind that filled the sails.

The ship began to turn away from the second star, back toward Never Land.

"Tricky. Take that!" James was mid-swing in his fight with Zarina. He looked up when the ship turned. "Blast it. The second star?! They turned the ship around."

"Yep!" Zarina said proudly. "We sure did."

As James continued to fight with the fairy, he called to his pirate crew, "Get this ship back on course!"

Vidia and Tink released a large hook tied to a rope above.

When the light was in Yang's eyes, Vidia swung down the rope, grabbing two swords from him as she soared past. At the wheel, she stabbed the swords through the ship's steering wheel, locking it in place. The boat could no longer turn.

"Bull's-eye!" Vidia cheered.

Furious, Yang grabbed some knives, his eyes tracking Vidia as she moved up a mast pole. "No fair. Come back here!" he shouted at her. "Fairies. Nothing but fairies. Stop moving so fast!"

Vidia mocked him from the top of the mast.

Yang hurled a dagger at her, but missed. "Jingle-jingle," he said in a poor imitation of fairy-speak. But his dagger didn't reach Vidia. Instead, it cut an important rope, holding back stacked barrels.

"Ohhhhh...uh-oh." Yang saw what he'd done.

SMASH. The barrels landed on top of him.

"Nice work," Tink complimented.

"Just thinking like a tinker." Vidia smiled.

The two of them flew off together to help their friends.

Rosetta was going up against Oppenheimer. He'd come up from the kitchen carrying everything he could find. "Take that, you little..." He threw china and kitchenware at her.

"Avast, crocky! Charge!" Rosetta rode the baby croc like she was on a horse going to war.

"Get it away, get it away, get it away now!" Oppenheimer shouted.

As the croc snapped at him, Oppenheimer continued to throw things at Rosetta. "No! Don't make me use my teaspoon! Oh no, oh, no you don't...you little..."

With Rosetta cheering, the croc forced

Oppenheimer backward, all the way to the ship's railing. The chef only had one thing left. It's his alarm clock. He tossed it and—CHOMP—the croc ate it.

"You ate my mummy's clock?!" Oppenheimer moaned. "What was wrong with the spatula?"

Rosetta fluttered off the croc, looking at him. "You ate his mummy's clock? Ya did?"

The croc grinned. His eyes ticktocked to the clock's beat. He licked his lips.

Rosetta laughed, then said, "Sic 'em!"

The croc lunged at Oppenheimer, knocking the chef to the railing. One last snap of the croc's sharp teeth, and they both fell overboard.

Rosetta looked over the side of the ship. "That's my crocky!"

James and Zarina continued to battle it out on the deck.

"There's nothing I revel in quite as much as a worthy opponent," James told her. Zarina managed a good blow that knocked James to his knees. "You're stronger than you look."

He popped back up and raised his sword.

While Zarina held her own, the other fairies went to release the anchor and stop the ship. It took all their strength, but they finally got it to move.

Iridessa said, "Anchors aweigh!"

"Grow some seaweed, Sunflower!" Rosetta called to Iridessa.

Iridessa jumped over the side of the ship. She made seaweed grow from the ocean floor, all around the anchor. The seaweed pulled back, and the boat was locked in place, hovering over the ocean. It jolted to a stop.

James stumbled backward before looking over the railing. "I've had just about enough of this!"

He grabbed a rope and swung out over the side of the ship. He cut the boat free from the seaweed. James cheered as the boat was set free.

The fairies were celebrating on the deck.

Suddenly a sail fell on top of them, trapping

them beneath. "Ha-ha!" James laughed, landing back on board and waving the knife he'd used to cut the sail's cord.

James tossed a knife at Zarina, who was still floating free. "You too!" It caught the hem of her dress and pinned her to the mast. He was winning, and he knew it.

"These ought to fetch a hefty price." Port wrapped the girls firmly in the fabric of the sail, and Starboard hung them, like a package, off the mast.

With one last glance at his captives, James returned to the helm. "Back on course!"

Zarina was struggling to break free.

Yang managed to get out from beneath the barrels, meeting up with Port and Starboard on deck.

With one last great effort, Zarina ripped her skirt and got away. She immediately flew to the top of the largest mast and untied the rope holding the sail.

James gasped as he saw the post swinging out and heading toward him. BAM! He was slammed away from the wheel and pinned against the central mast.

Zarina swooped in and took back the vial of Blue Dust.

"Give me that dust! NO!" James reached desperately for her.

She strapped the dust to her chest, then darted to the helm and pushed a lever. Zarina spun the wheel furiously. The boat began to tip.

James and the pirates were slipping toward the side. "Aaaaaahhh!" the men shouted as they went overboard.

Zarina let the boat flip until it was nearly upside down. The golden dust that the pirates had put in the crow's nest poured out. "The dust! Not my dust! No..." James reached for it, with two hands, trying to collect the precious flakes. He fell from the mast and plummeted downward, disappearing in a swirl of golden dust.

The ship tilted back to a normal position in the sky as Zarina went to free her friends.

"I got the dust!" she told them.

"You're okay," Tink breathed.

"Oh, thank goodness," Rosetta said.

"Let's get you out of there." She was about to free the fairies when James appeared over the side of the boat.

She was shocked to see him flying. He grinned.

"Lean right, fly right..." He grabbed the Blue Dust back from Zarina. "I'll take that."

"Noo!" Zarina pulled out her sword, then followed close behind.

"Now, where was I? Ah yes." He took his place at the ship's wheel, hanging the Blue Dust vial back around his neck. In a flash, Zarina had taken the vial again. But in the escape, she was flung back against the rigging, and the vial fell from her hand.

Both James and Zarina reached for it. James got there first. "Hiyaaa!" He blocked her with his sword and grabbed it.

Without a captain at the wheel, the ship suddenly lurched. The boat turned itself around, heading back to the second star.

Zarina managed to grab the vial again, but James got it back right away.

Trapped in the bag, the girls watched everything.

James and Zarina played tug-of-war with the vial. The cord snapped, and the vial was flung up the mast. The vial landed on the rigging.

Zarina got there first, but the cord was stuck. As she tugged on it, she noticed the second star getting closer. "The second star," she breathed.

James flew up to the rigging, grabbing a metal hook on his way. Zarina tried to fly away, but James grabbed the cord with the hook and swatted the fairy with the flat of his blade. She lost control, and the vial landed between them.

James snagged it and stood tall. "You fought well, little fairy. But it's over. The dust is mine.

The ship is mine. Your adventure has come to an end."

Zarina felt defeated, but then she saw a glimmer. A speck of spilled Blue Pixie Dust lay close enough to touch. She reached out....

"Oh, go ahead. Take it." James laughed as if the dust was worthless. "What's one speck between friends?"

Zarina looked at how he was covered with golden dust. "No, really. I think you should have it all," she said, then threw the speck of Blue Dust at him. Just as it had in the Blue Dust Vault with her bracelet back in Pixie Hollow, the Blue Dust caused the golden dust on James to multiply.

"From a trickle to a roar...." Zarina repeated what Fairy Gary had said to her that day.

A moment later, James was zooming all around the ship, completely out of control. The Blue Dust vial fell. Zarina caught it. His body hit the mast, freeing the fairies.

They gathered together to watch as James,

106

still coated with golden dust, flopped over the side of the ship and flew wildly out to sea, still clutching the Blue Dust vial.

"Look at him go," Rosetta said.

"He's very fast," Silvermist remarked.

"Yeah? You think?" Vidia snickered.

"Time to get that Blue Dust back?" Zarina asked Tink.

"Watch this," Tink replied.

Using her water talent, Tink created a giant wave that caused the other pirates to clamor. James slammed through the wave and came out wet, the golden dust dripping off his body.

"Can't fly when you're wet," Zarina told James as she flew over to him. She snagged the Blue Dust vial from him. He hung in the air for a split second before...

SPLASH. He fell out of the sky and hit the water below.

Tink snapped her fingers, and the wave disappeared.

"Good-bye, James," Zarina said before she and

Tink returned to the ship.

Out in the water, James was floating, surrounded by his crew. "Curse you, fairies!" he shouted, waving a fist toward the girls.

"Tiny she-devils they are, really," Oppenheimer said.

A ticktock sound interrupted James's screaming and shouting. The crocodile, with the chef's clock in his belly, swam toward him, mad and hungry.

James swam away as fast as he could with the croc close behind, snapping at him. "I'm not a codfish! I'm a pirate!"

The girls were thrilled to see the pirates gone.

"We did it!" Tink said.

"It's over!" Iridessa clapped her hands.

"You got the dust!" Fawn congratulated Zarina.

"We can go home!" Silvermist smiled.

"I am gonna soak in a nice, hot milkweed bath," Rosetta said. "Get the smell o' pirate off me."

Zarina fluttered to the side, not joining in the celebration. She gave the bottle of Blue Pixie Dust to Tinker Bell. "Please take this back to Pixie Hollow."

Tink took it, but she was a bit confused. "Zarina," she said. "We didn't just come for the dust."

The girls all smiled at her, opening their circle to welcome her. Zarina rushed to them, and they all hugged.

They were ready to go when Fawn pulled Rosetta to the side. "Um, Ro? There's something you should know." She said quickly, "It's about your hair."

The girls disappeared over the side of the ship.

Rosetta screamed. "First I lose my talent, then I become a mother, I do-si-do'd in a stinky shoe, and now my hair! Argggh!"

Chapter Ten

The girls sailed the pirate ship back to Pixie Hollow feeling happier than ever before.

"Hang on, guys," Vidia announced. She was steering the boat.

"There it is." Silvermist could see the lights ahead.

"Home." Vidia smiled.

When they arrived, Clank was still pedaling the snowmaker like he'd been instructed. He was exhausted. He looked up to see the pirate ship.

Aboard, Zarina and Silvermist flew in circles above the crow's nest, creating new special vats of pixie dust. Then, at Zarina's command, Iridessa and Rosetta pulled a giant lever. Pixie dust floated into the amphitheater.

Silvermist created a wind to blow the dust onto the crowd.

Slowly, the fairies began to wake up.

"Bobble! You're awake!" Clank gave his friend a huge hug.

"I was asleep?" Bobble yawned.

THUNK! The ship dropped anchor. The girls waved to the crowd.

"I think this is the best show yet!" Gliss told Peri.

Queen Clarion, Lord Milori, the ministers, and Fairy Mary looked at one another, then up to the ship.

The girls flew down into the stadium.

Queen Clarion went to meet them halfway. "Girls...?" She wanted an explanation.

Tink moved forward. "Queen Clarion, we got the Blue Dust back." She handed the Blue Dust vial to the queen.

"Which I didn't know was missing," she said, wrinkling her forehead.

"We also got Zarina." Tink fluttered aside so the queen could see.

"Well then, the Blue Dust isn't the most valuable thing you've brought me today," the queen said.

Zarina was grateful for the welcome. Tink smiled.

Fairy Gary came rushing up. "Zarina?"

Zarina stepped back nervously, but Gary grabbed her and spun her around happily. "You're home."

"As for pixie dust..." Zarina wanted to tell him the whole story.

"As for pixie dust, she's really mastered that thing of hers," Tink interrupted Zarina.

"She even grew a Pixie Dust Tree," Rosetta put in.

"Now we've got an extra!" Silvermist said.

Fairy Gary considered what they were telling him, then asked, "A second Pixie Dust Tree? Does this talent of yours have a name?"

"Alchemy." Zarina got a twinkle in her eye.

"Pixie dust alchemy."

"You should really see her in action," Tink told everyone.

"Well..." Queen Clarion looked around at all the fairies in the amphitheater. "We do have an audience."

Zarina was ready to show everyone what she could do.

The stage was set for a new performance.

Fireflies formed a circle, creating a spotlight over a music box on the stage.

Clank blew his horn.

"Wooohoohoohoohoo!" Bobble cheered.

Queen Clarion and Fairy Mary were in their seats, waiting for the show to begin.

The gears of the music box turned. When the top popped open, the fairies came onto the stage. Zarina was in the middle. She pulled several pouches from her pocket and tossed some dust on Tink. Suddenly, Tink's dress turned green—

she was a tinker again.

"Thanks!" Tink said, and got into position near the music box.

Zarina tossed another handful of dust onto Rosetta. Not only was her dress now back to pink, but her hair had grown back. "Well, how's my hair?" Rosetta asked.

"It's good," Fawn said.

Rosetta laughed as she flew over the top of the music box. Flower stems burst upward as the music grew louder.

Next was Fawn. A little dust turned her outfit back to orange. She whipped her hair and did a backflip. "Yeah."

Tink moved some levers.

A panel on the music box opened, and Fawn flew upward, followed by a playful flock of orange butterflies.

Another lever opened another panel. Silvermist turned blue again. She raised a stream of water. It spiraled behind her like a ribbon.

Next, Iridessa spun into a cloud of dust that

brought back her yellow glow. She reflected the wide moonbeam through a diamond ring and ornate mirrors, creating a beautiful rainbow within Silvermist's water spheres.

It was amazing.

Finally, Vidia was showered with dust, and her dress turned to purple.

"All right!" Vidia zoomed around Tink's box, spinning the mirrors faster and faster. The light beams danced across the audience like a disco ball.

"Gorgeous," Fairy Mary said.

The girls took their bows.

The show was fantastic.

Zarina had created magic.

Beyond Pixie Hollow, a black-and-red ship sailed in the water toward Never Land. The ship was flying the Jolly Roger.

"Man in the water," a pirate named Smee announced to the crew.

James was floating, hanging on to a broken mast.

"Oh, dear! Oh, my!" Mr. Smee noticed the pirate's hand. "Ohh...that's a very nice hook!"

James, his black hair a mess of wet, tangled curls, used the hook to pull himself up.

He looked toward Pixie Hollow with anger in his eyes and groaned, "Just give me a hand."

The End

Read more
Disney Fairies adventures!

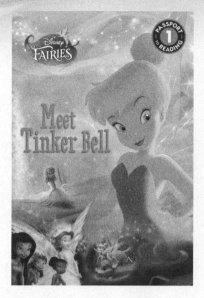

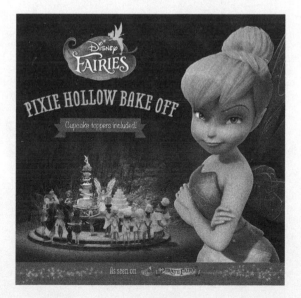